Adaptation by Justine Fontes

Illustrations by MADA Design, Inc.

Meredith® Books

Des Moines, Iowa

Welcome to New Hive City! This is where bees make honey. It's what bees do. It's all bees do. All but one bee that is—Barry wants to explore the world outside of the buzzing hive!

Find these things:

camera

glasses

honey test tube

busy bee

wastebasket

honey tank

sign

desk

Barry goes on a mission with the pollen jocks. The world outside the hive is bright and colorful, but it's a dangerous place to be a bee.

Find these things:

football

birds

hot dog

Mooseblood

pollen jock

kite

biker

dog

Barry meets Vanessa, and they become fast friends. One day while shopping, Barry sees shelf after shelf full of honey. "What is this?" Barry asks, surprised. "Humans are stealing our honey!"

Find these things:

pinwheel

honey

honey dripper

sale sign

advertisement

candy

rose

store magazine

Barry decides to sue the humans for stealing the bees' honey. So Vanessa helps Barry prepare for the court case at her flower shop.

Find these things:

rose

bird of paradise

daisy

plant

book

basket

mug

greeting cards

Barry and Vanessa enjoy a friendly dinner while talking about the court case. This little bee is about to make a big change in the world.

Find these things:

candle

magazine

fashion magazine

flowerpot

fork

salt and pepper

vase

table

Barry wins the court case against the humans. All of the honey in the world returns to the bees!

Find these things:

camera

daisy

flag

mircrophone

rose

sign

honey bottle

candy

No longer needed to pollinate and make honey, the bees are now busy playing and having fun. New Hive City is the place to be a bee!

Find these things:

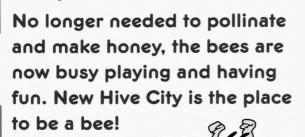
coaster bee

slider bee

skateboarder bee

basketball bees

picnic bee

juggler bee

ice cream bee

motorcycle bee

Since the bees stopped working and pollinating, all the flowers have started to die. Barry and Vanessa have an idea. The Rose Parade is the last chance to save the world from being flowerless.

Find these things:

parasol

soda

plane

kid

hat

two dogs

sticker

flower

After borrowing a float full of flowers, Barry and Vanessa catch a flight back home. Barry must take over flying the plane with a lift from his bee friends.

Find these things:

passenger

bird

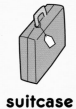
bird-of-paradise

hat

suitcase

PLEASE DON'T
BOTHER
THE PILOTS

sign

pollen jocks

car

Thanks to the busy bees, the
flowers are in full bloom. The
world looks rosy again!

Find these things:

hat

headbands

bird

dog

kid

bag

car

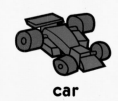

backpack